Animals of Africa

WARTHOGS

by Nancy Furstinger

FOCUS READERS

FOCUS READERS

www.focusreaders.com

Focus Readers is distributed by North Star Editions:
sales@northstareditions.com | 888-417-0195

Produced for Focus Readers by Red Line Editorial.

Photographs ©: Travel Stock/Shutterstock Images, cover, 1; Jan van Biljon/Shutterstock Images, 4–5; Red Line Editorial, 6; EcoPic/iStockphoto, 8–9; Jixin YU/Shutterstock Images, 10; JJMaree/iStockphoto, 12; thespecialistsa/iStockphoto, 14–15; Susan Schmitz/Shutterstock Images, 16; znm/iStockphoto, 17; Uwe-Bergwitz/iStockphoto, 18; Jonathan Pledger/Shutterstock Images, 20; Astarphotographer/iStockphoto, 22 (top left); mattwicks/iStockphoto, 22 (top right); Aaron Amat/Shutterstock Images, 22 (bottom left), 29; stray_cat/iStockphoto, 22 (bottom right); Rudi Hulshof/Shutterstock Images, 24; Photo used with kind permission from Imire Rhino and Wildlife Conservation, Zimbabwe - www.imire.co.zwr, 27

ISBN
978-1-63517-268-3 (hardcover)
978-1-63517-333-8 (paperback)
978-1-63517-463-2 (ebook pdf)
978-1-63517-398-7 (hosted ebook)

Library of Congress Control Number: 2017935118

Printed in the United States of America
Mankato, MN
June, 2017

About the Author

Nancy Furstinger is the author of more than 100 books. She has been a feature writer for a daily newspaper, a managing editor of trade and consumer magazines, and an editor at children's book publishing houses. She lives in upstate New York with a menagerie of animals.

TABLE OF CONTENTS

CHAPTER 1

HOME ON THE SAVANNA

Warthogs roam the **savannas** of Africa. Here warthogs have everything they need to survive. Grass and plants cover this open space. These plants can grow even during a **drought**.

Savannas often have tall grasses.

Warthogs live in many areas of Africa.

A warthog's **habitat** is hot and dry. But warthogs know how to keep cool. They find mud to **wallow** in. A mud bath cools them down during scorching days.

FUN FACT

Warthogs can live without water for several months.

Sometimes warthogs go underground to rest. They use **burrows** made by other animals. Burrows provide a cool spot to nap out of the hot sun.

At night, the savanna gets cold. Warthogs huddle together in their burrows. They use their body heat to keep one another warm.

CHAPTER 2

WARTY PIGS

Warthogs are wild pigs. They have **warts** on their heads. This is how they got their name. Long bristles on the warts form beards. Male warthogs have four warts. Female warthogs have only two.

Warthogs are related to pigs, but their warts make them look very different.

Warthogs have thin fur.

A warthog is mostly bald. Its skin is gray or black. On its back is a thick **mane**. The mane runs from the top of the warthog's head down the middle of its back.

A warthog's head is shaped like a shovel. It has a snout. In its mouth are four **tusks**. The two lower tusks are short and sharp. The two upper tusks are long and curved.

FUN FACT

Pilots nicknamed a US Air Force plane the Warthog. This plane was ugly and tough.

A warthog runs across the savanna.

FUN FACT

Warthogs stick their tails up in the air when they run. The bristles at the end wave like flags.

Warthogs weigh approximately 185 pounds (84 kg). Their big bodies are shaped like barrels. Warthogs' legs are long compared with other pigs' legs. Their hooves have four toes. Warthogs can run fast. They are able to run up to 30 miles per hour (48 km/h).

CHAPTER 3

DIGGING AND FIGHTING

Warthogs are built for digging. They use their snouts like bulldozers. This helps them uproot plant bulbs. Warthogs also use their upper tusks to dig. They use their sharp front teeth to **graze**.

A warthog searches the ground for food.

PARTS OF A WARTHOG

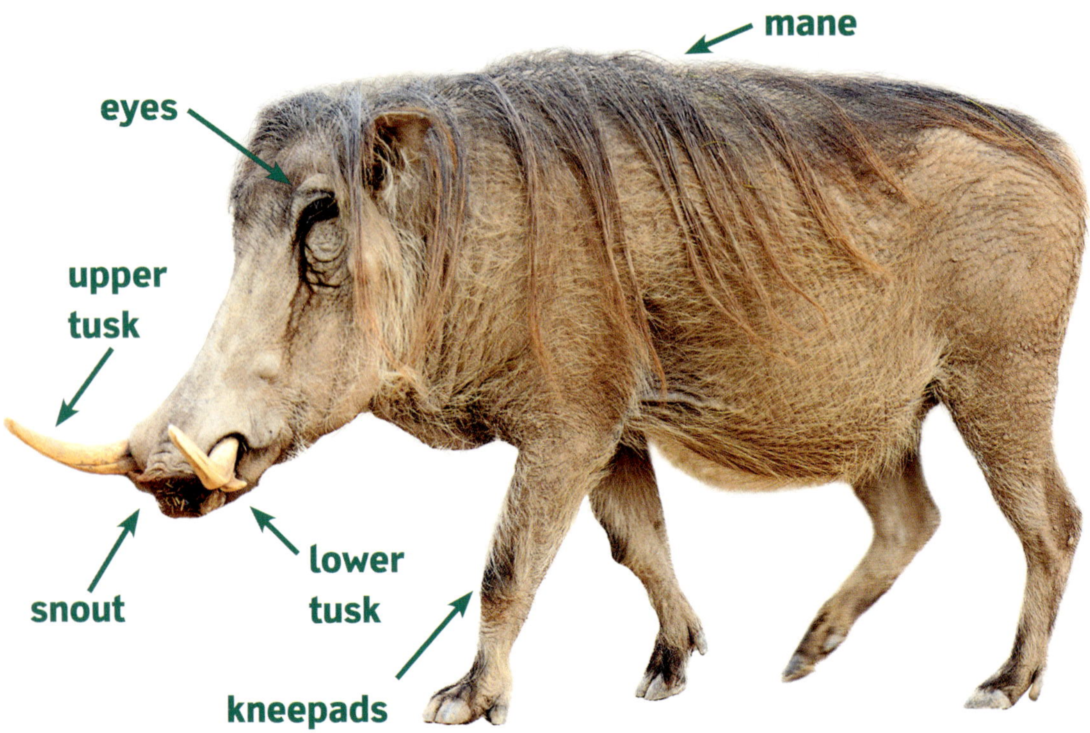

Thick skin protects the animal's front knees. The skin acts like kneepads. Warthogs often kneel while eating grass. Kneepads help

A warthog kneels to eat grass.

them do this for long periods. Warthogs can also shuffle on their knees to new feeding spots.

Warthogs must lower their heads to graze. This body position puts them in danger of **predators**.

Warthogs squeal loudly when fighting.

It is hard to defend against predators. But warthogs' eyes are on the sides of their heads. The eyes are set high up and far back.

This lets warthogs keep a lookout for predators while grazing.

Sometimes male warthogs fight one another. The males use their curved tusks in battle. Their tusks form a semicircle. They can grow up to 35 inches (89 cm) long.

FUN FACT

Warts protect males during fights. They act like armor by shielding the animal's eyes and jaws.

CHAPTER 4

LIFE IN A SOUNDER

After the males finish fighting, the winner of a battle gets his pick of females for a mate. Then he tries to impress his female. He does this by strutting sideways. He tries to look strong.

A male warthog must show off after a fight.

WARTHOG LIFE CYCLE

A female can have many piglets.

Piglets nurse for five weeks.

Males leave their mothers after 15 months. Females stay in the sounder.

Warthogs live for approximately 15 years.

Male warthogs are known as boars. Female warthogs are called sows. Sows have newborns in burrows. Two sows might share the same home. Newborn warthogs are called piglets. Sows and piglets live together in groups. These groups are called sounders.

FUN FACT

Warthogs use many different sounds. They grunt, snort, and growl when alarmed.

Most sows have two or three piglets at a time. But they can have as many as eight.

Sows protect their piglets from enemies. A mother warthog backs up into her burrow. Her head blocks the entrance. She keeps a lookout for predators. She uses her tusks to defend against cheetahs, crocodiles, lions, and leopards.

Newborn piglets drink milk from their mothers. Later they will graze. Warthogs are herbivores. They eat grasses and berries. They eat bark and roots, too.

THAT'S AMAZING!

UNLIKELY FRIENDS

A warthog piglet named Poggle had two odd playmates. The warthog's best friends were a black rhino and a hyena. All three young animals lived at a wildlife **preserve**. People rescued the animals after their parents died.

Poggle and his buddies ate breakfast inside their caretaker's house. Then they explored the bush together. They chased one another. They splashed in the mud. Later, all three napped in the garden.

Soon the trio grew big enough to be released. They needed to live among their own species.

Poggle meets Tatenda the rhino.

FOCUS ON
WARTHOGS

Write your answers on a separate sheet of paper.

1. Write a letter to a friend describing the main ideas of Chapter 3.
2. Would you like to observe warthogs at a game reserve? Why or why not?
3. Which shape matches a warthog's head?
   - **A.** barrel
   - **B.** semicircle
   - **C.** shovel
4. What might happen if a sow did not guard her burrow?
   - **A.** A boar might move into the burrow.
   - **B.** A predator might eat a piglet.
   - **C.** The burrow might flood.

5. What does **uproot** mean in this book?

Warthogs are built for digging. They use their snouts like bulldozers. This helps them ***uproot*** *plant bulbs.*

- **A.** to pull something out of the ground
- **B.** to bury something deep underground
- **C.** to create a tall pile

6. What does **herbivores** mean in this book?

Warthogs are ***herbivores****. They eat grasses and berries. They eat bark and roots, too.*

- **A.** animals that eat only meat
- **B.** animals that eat only plants
- **C.** animals that eat meat and plants

Answer key on page 32.

GLOSSARY

burrows
Holes or tunnels dug by small animals.

drought
A period of dry weather.

graze
To eat small bits of food throughout the day.

habitat
The type of place where plants or animals normally grow or live.

mane
The hair that grows on the necks or backs of some animals.

predators
Animals that hunt other animals for food.

preserve
An area of land set aside for managing and protecting animals.

savannas
Grasslands with few or no trees.

tusks
Long, pointed teeth that stick out from the faces of some animals.

wallow
To roll around in something.

warts
Lump on the skin.

TO LEARN MORE

BOOKS

Loy, Jessica. *Weird & Wild Animal Facts.* New York: Henry Holt and Company, 2015.

Owen, Ruth. *Warthogs.* New York: Windmill Books, 2014.

Spelman, Lucy. *National Geographic Animal Encyclopedia.* Washington, DC: National Geographic, 2012.

NOTE TO EDUCATORS

Visit **www.focusreaders.com** to find lesson plans, activities, links, and other resources related to this title.

INDEX

Answer Key: 1. Answers will vary; **2.** Answers will vary; **3.** C; **4.** B; **5.** A; **6.** B